Obl. Davis Kidd   9.00

MW01234489

Understanding Issues

Child Abuse

Gail B. Stewart

KIDHAVEN PRESS™

San Diego • Detroit • New York • San Francisco • Cleveland
New Haven, Conn. • Waterville, Maine • London • Munich

LIBRARY OF CONGRESS CATALOGING-IN-PUBLICATION DATA

Stewart, Gail B., 1949–
    Child abuse / By Gail B. Stewart.
        p. cm. — (Understanding issues)
    Summary: Using real-life examples, discusses why parents hurt or neglect their
children, why children often don't tell anyone they are being abused, and what
can be done about the widespread and dangerous problem of child abuse.
Includes bibliographical references.
        ISBN 0-7377-1280-5 (hardback : alk. paper)
    1. Child abuse—Juvenile literature. [1. Child abuse.] I. Title. II. Series.
    HV6626.5 .S74   2003
    362.76—dc21

    2002002164

Contents

Chapter One
A National Disgrace 4

Chapter Two
Why Do They Do It? 13

Chapter Three
"You Never Forget" 23

Chapter Four
Fighting Against Abuse 33

Notes 41

Glossary 43

For Further Exploration 44

Index 45

Picture Credits 47

About the Author 48

A National Disgrace

Jan (not her real name) remembers the afternoon she hit her son. "We were coming home from daycare," she says. "Mark was four. I was getting him buckled up in the car, and he started chattering about how much he liked it there. He liked the toys and he liked the kids. He liked the lunch that they made for him.

"I was really tired and crabby from working all day. I had spilled ink on my new blouse. I had a headache, too. Anyway, I asked Mark if he liked the daycare place better than his own home. He said, 'Yeah, I think so.'"

"I Know That Was Wrong"

Jan's eyes filled with tears as she recounted the event. "I wanted him to say that he liked our house better, I think. It was a mean question to ask him— he was just excited about the toys and the new kids to play with. But I was just looking for a fight, I guess. So anyway, I stopped the car and I slapped him. I hit him three or four times, right in a row."

The terrible pain of child abuse can usually be seen on the faces of its victims.

"I know that was wrong," she says as she continues crying. "He screamed and cried and put his hands up around his face. He wanted me to stop; he yelled 'Daddy, Daddy.' And I felt so awful, so ashamed."

Jan says that Mark's face was red and sore. "You could see the red mark in the shape of my hand," she says. "And he was bleeding a little by his eyebrow, where my ring cut him. I thought, what kind of a mother am I, that would hurt her kid like this?"[1]

"A Misuse of Power"

Jan knows that she made a very bad mistake. What she did is called **child abuse**—hurting or causing harm to a child. "It is a misuse of power," says one counselor. "Parents, teachers, babysitters, daycare workers—we all are stronger and more powerful than children. We are supposed to use that power, that strength, to teach and protect them. Not to punch, slap, kick, or shake them."[2]

Child abuse is a big problem in the United States. In 1985 about 1.4 million cases of child abuse were reported. In 1997 the number had more than doubled—3 million cases. Counselors say that there are at least that many cases that were not reported. No one really knows how much more abuse is happening every day.

Bad things can happen to children who are abused. Some children are badly bruised; others might suffer burns or broken bones. An estimated four thousand children—many of them babies—die each year from abuse. It is, say experts, a national disgrace.

Defining Abuse

Sometimes the term "child abuse" can be tricky to understand. "Hurting" and "abuse" are not always the same thing. Sometimes some very good parents hurt their children. For instance, when two-year-old Ted burned his arm on the backyard grill, his parents rushed him to the hospital.

A child forced to live in filth may be considered abused.

The doctor told them that the little boy would be fine as long as the burn did not get infected. To keep this from happening, Ted's parents had to wash the area three times each day with special soap and warm water.

This was good medical advice. However, having his arm washed was very painful for Ted. His parents tried to explain why they needed to wash the burn, but he screamed and cried. He tried to pull his arm away. Even though this hurt Ted, it was not abuse. They were not injuring their little boy. They were trying to make sure that he got well.

"It's Almost Like You Never Been a Kid Yourself"

However, what Lee was doing was definitely child abuse. For almost two years, his wife Mary says, he abused their small children. He was impatient with

Sadness shows on the faces of three brothers, one with a black eye.

them and found them annoying. He thought they made too much noise and asked too many questions, Mary remembers. "I told him once that he never laughed," she says. "I said, 'Lee, it's almost like you never been a kid yourself, the way you are with these kids.'

"He would hit the kids—especially when I wasn't home. . . . He'd throw shoes at them, hit them with the broom handle. He'd punish them all the time over little things that didn't need more than a scolding. And he'd pinch their hands, too, right on the palms. That hurt them like anything. He had big, hard hands, and those kids would cry. They were little, after all."[3]

Everybody Pays

Although most people do not abuse children, all Americans pay for it. About $94 billion each year is needed to pay for the damage done by adults who abuse children. Some of the money goes to doctors and hospitals to help children heal. Some money is used to build shelters where abused children can stay when their homes are not safe.

Tony, age fourteen, is staying in such a shelter for a while. His father drinks too much and often gets angry. Not long ago, Tony's father hit Tony and knocked out two of his teeth. Police officers came to the house and took Tony to the shelter.

"I didn't have time to be scared," he says. "I went to the hospital and I got stitches in my mouth.

When drunk, alcoholic parents may abuse or neglect their children.

And I stayed there overnight. Then I came here, to St. Joe's. I still live here. There are a lot of kids—all different ages. There are teachers here, and we have school every day. But I really don't mind it. It's better than being home when my dad is drinking."[4]

Meanwhile
Children at shelters also have counselors and **therapists**. These are people who specialize in healing the damage inside—the fear, anger, and mistrust

that abused children often feel. Counselors and therapists also need to work with abusers. They help teach parents and others who abuse children to control their angry feelings.

Drawing can help children express their feelings about being abused.

But the problem is serious and widespread. "Overwhelming is the word I'd use," says one counselor. "Millions of cases reported each year, and who knows how many that aren't? Millions of kids—from newborn babies to teenagers—that are being hurt by people they trust to take care of them. It's something we have to change."[5]

Chapter Two

Why Do They Do It?

Some people think that parents who abuse children are crazy. But that is not true. Counselors who work with abusers know that most seem quite normal. They do not act like monsters or criminals. It would be difficult to pick an abuser out of a crowd of people.

Abusers are found among every race and every religion. And it is not only poor people who abuse their children. Child abusers are among the middle class and the rich, too. There is simply no way to know just by looking at someone.

A Number of Causes

There are a number of reasons why parents abuse their children. Some parents are angry and frustrated at things in their own lives. Some feel angry about their jobs. Others are angry because they do not have enough money to pay the bills. And others were abused themselves as children.

Sometimes their anger gets out of control, and they lash out. Unfortunately, an angry parent sometimes lashes out at the wrong person. Sometimes it is the child who becomes the target, even if that child has done nothing wrong. One man says that he could not handle stress. At work his boss often scolded him, and that made him angry. He did not want to confront his boss, for fear that he might get fired. So he found other people to get mad at instead.

"I remember driving home from work," he says. "I'd honk at people and yell at other drivers. I was mad. And then I'd get home and my kids are running around. I would lose it—just lose control. What started off as a spanking turned into punching sometimes."[6]

Teaching a Lesson

Lisa says that her boyfriend was the same way. He had never learned to control his anger. Instead, he sometimes seemed to explode, getting angry at the wrong people. When Lisa was not home to supervise, her boyfriend hurt her children. "He'd beat them for [playing and being silly]," she says. "He'd take a toilet brush, you know, with the bristles? He'd hit them over and over on their legs until they were bruised and had bloody scratches all over them."[7]

Doctors see many small children who have been abused by parents trying to "teach" them a lesson.

In 1954, police in Texas discovered this boy's parents
had chained him to his bed.

One little eighteen-month-old girl was brought to the emergency room in Los Angeles. "She had cigarette burns all over her face and arms," says the doctor. "She was frightened and hurt—she wouldn't even look at me. . . . I asked the father what had happened.

"He told me that she kept wanting to touch the lighter that was on the coffee table. He said he kept telling her, 'No, it's hot.' The father said he finally started burning her so she would understand 'hot' and leave his lighter alone."[8]

"You Ignore Kids, That's Abuse"

Many cases of child abuse happen because of drug abuse, too. Sometimes the abuse is physical. Sometimes—especially with drug users—the abuse is **neglect**. Neglect means that the parent does not pay attention to what the child needs. Neglected children are often hungry. The little ones have soiled diapers that have not been changed. In cold weather, they are not dressed in warm clothes. If the parents are abusing drugs, they often ignore their children. They may leave them alone in the house, with no babysitter. They do not hold their children or play with them.

Trina is an example of a parent who used to neglect her children. As a mother of three small children, she was addicted to **crack**. With no money and no place to live, Trina and her boyfriend lived with his grandmother.

"That lady was a drug addict herself," says Trina. "Always people there, coming and going, selling it, using it. For a whole month, I didn't do anything else except use crack. . . . I look back on that time and I feel real bad about it."

Although she did not hit her children during that time, Trina admits that she abused them. "You ignore kids, that's abuse," she admits. "It's hurting them same as hitting them, only it doesn't show. But I didn't give those kids attention. I didn't feed them, I just used crack. I spent my whole welfare check up . . . my kids were starving for something

A sad, bruised girl crouches in fear.

A girl cries out as her father prepares to take drugs.

to eat . . . I remember my kids crying at me all the time, trying to climb in my lap, but I just pushed them away, told them to get away."[9]

Too Young to Have Children

Counselors know that one problem is the large number of teenage girls having babies and keeping them. Even though they may be only thirteen or fourteen years old, some pregnant teens like the

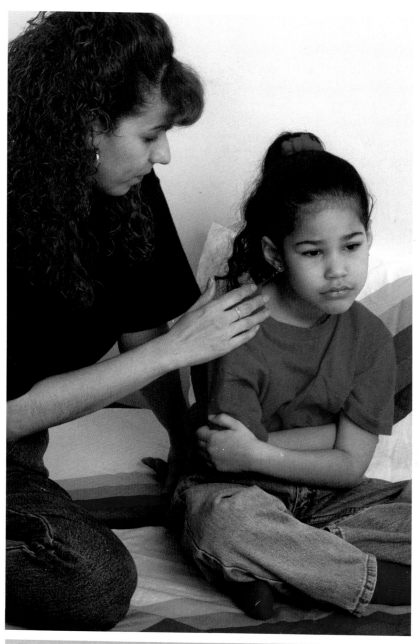

For a healthy relationship, parents must learn to listen and talk to their children.

idea of having a baby of their own. But they are not ready for the hard work of having a baby.

"The idea of having a little baby, like a doll, is very appealing," says one counselor. "A little person, who will love them totally—what a great feeling! But as the months go by and these little babies are up at night with sore gums from teething, or earaches, or whatever—they become less appealing to their mothers."[10]

When this happens, many teens get angry or bored. They may feel resentful. They wonder why they should sit at home with a crying baby when their friends are having fun.

"I Just Forgot"

Dorie, a seventeen-year-old teen mother, felt this way. Her baby sometimes had stomachaches and cried during the night. It made her nervous being in the apartment with a baby that screamed all the time. She tried holding him and feeding him. But nothing seemed to make him feel better. After a while, she left him in his crib and closed the door. She turned up the television, too. At least she could not hear him as well, she thought.

A friend called and asked her to go to a party. At first she said no, but then she changed her mind. Dorie could not afford a babysitter. She went out, leaving the baby at home. She says that she thought about him at first, but she was having fun with her old friends. "We were partying," she says. "I meant to call my sister, to have her look in on him. She lives like a few blocks away. But she wasn't home when I called, and after that, I just forgot about [the baby]."[11]

Luckily, her neighbors called the police. They had heard the baby crying; they knocked on the door, but Dorie was not home. The police came, and they opened the apartment. The baby was

Teenage parents often do not realize how challenging it is to raise a child until they have one.

barely alive; he had stopped crying hours before. He had not eaten. His skin was covered in sores from his dirty diaper. Another few hours, one medical worker said, and the baby would have died from neglect.

The Hurting Goes On

Stories like these are difficult to read. It seems impossible to imagine how people could hurt children in so many ways—for so many reasons. But police, doctors, and others who try to help abused children know that there is more to their stories. Children hurt from abuse long after their bruises or broken bones heal.

What happens to children after they have been abused? How do they handle the fear of being hurt again? Counselors know that abused children will be affected by the abuse for years afterward—in a variety of ways.

Chapter Three

"You Never Forget"

Eight-year-old Joseph told his teacher that his back burned. She lifted the back of his shirt and saw why. His back was covered with the worst bruises and welts she had ever seen. The teacher was shocked, and she asked Joseph what had happened.

"If You Tell, I'll Get It Again"

But Joseph did not want to tell her at first. Finally, he said that his father whipped him with an extension cord. His father had done it many times before, too. But Joseph told his teacher that she could not tell anyone else. "If you tell," he said, "I'll get it again."[12]

Many children are fearful after they have been abused. Adults who abuse children know that what they have done is wrong. They could be arrested and put in jail. To make sure no one finds out about the abuse, they threaten the children. When thirteen-year-old Kadee left a gate open by mistake, her father kicked her over and over while she lay on the

Abusive parents can be arrested and sent to jail.

ground crying. He had been wearing cowboy boots, and her injuries were severe.

"I didn't go to school for a week," she says. "My father wouldn't let me—my arms and my neck were bruised. And when I did go back, he made me wear jeans and a turtleneck. It was May, and it was hot. I felt stupid, because the other kids were wearing shorts and stuff. He told me that if I told anybody at school, he'd find out. And he'd kick me worse the next time. So I didn't tell anybody. At least, not that time."[13]

Threats

Child abuse victims are afraid for other reasons, too. Many worry that if they tell someone about the abuse, they will be taken from their parents. For a lot of children, this is as scary as being beaten.

Two filthy, neglected girls sit in the hallway of their home.

Jerry was five and still wet his bed sometimes. This made his stepfather furious, and the stepfather hit Jerry's bare bottom with a belt. The metal on the belt left bloody marks, and his stepfather warned him not to tell his kindergarten teacher.

"He said that if I told, I'd get taken away and put in a different home," says Jerry, now nine. "He said that I'd have a different mother and father, and I'd never get to see my own mom again. So I was really scared that someone would find out about my getting whipped. I didn't care if I ever saw [my stepfather] again, but I was really afraid to lose my mom."[14]

"We Couldn't Tell Anybody"

Young children are terrified of their family being split apart. Even older children worry about being put into a shelter or a temporary foster home. Sometimes, they know, a temporary home might be in a different part of town. That could mean a different school, and separation from their friends.

Allie, fourteen, knew that his mother was neglecting him and his little brothers. She was drinking and smoking marijuana. She was never home when her sons came home from school. She stayed out very late, too. Often several days would go by without their seeing her at all. Allie did not want anyone to find out. He worried that he and his brothers would be separated and put in different homes.

"Our house was real messy, really bad," he says. "I knew that we couldn't tell anybody what was going on. The teachers were getting kind of suspicious. She hadn't turned in all these forms for school—they were all in a pile on the counter. Every day I'd tell my teacher that I forgot, or that Mom was sick, or something.

"So finally I told [my brothers] that they couldn't say anything about Mom at school or to their friends.

Signs of Possible Child Abuse

The child . . .

- Has had many unusual or unexplainable injuries.

- Seems sad and cries a lot.

- Fights with classmates or destroys things.

- Is violent toward pets.

- Seems tired and has nightmares.

- Seems afraid of parents.

- Does not want to go home after school, as if afraid of something there.

Source: American Academy of Pediatrics.

I just started signing stuff, signing her name. And when the phone rang, when someone would ask for my mom, I'd say she was at work."[15]

Running from Abuse

Many older abused children simply run away. In fact, a 1999 survey on homeless teens found that more than 80 percent said that abuse was the reason they ran away. "Why should you just stay and keep taking it?" says Jenny, a runaway. "It's going to be one more black eye, one more bloody lip, or worse. I'd rather be on my own."[16]

But those who run quickly find a lot of new problems on the streets. Food is expensive and money does not last long. Some steal, some sell drugs, and some become prostitutes. Counselors say that because these young runaways are not used to being on their own, they are in danger. They are more likely to use drugs. They are also more likely to be the victim of a dangerous crime—even murder.

"I've been shot at, been colder than anyone would believe possible, and had to eat food out of dumpsters," admits one fourteen-year-old who ran away because of abuse. "It's a nightmare out there, that's a fact."[17]

Trouble Later On

There are a number of ways that abuse can affect children as they grow into adults. Many have trouble trusting other people. They may find it hard to

Some children run away to the streets to avoid abuse at home.

make close friendships. They may find dating especially difficult, too.

"It's a trust thing," says one man. "I was abused by my stepfather when I was about nine. I didn't have any feelings for him, but I was really hurt that my mom didn't stop the abuse. She knew, but she just let him.

"That loss of trust was a big deal, and I think a lot of abuse victims feel it. Even now that I'm in my 30s. It's hard for me to completely feel that I can trust people. And I have times when I feel that I'm not as good as other people.

Abused children can grow up to be abusive adults.

"I lack confidence. That's something I feel a lot—on the job, with other people. And with me, it goes back to the same thing. If my own parent didn't protect me when I was nine, how good could I have been?"[18]

The Cycle

This lack of confidence and low self-esteem can have another effect, too. Abused children who have low opinions of themselves often become abusers when they grow up. They will often mistreat their own children as they were once mistreated.

One counselor says that she has worked with hundreds of adults who abuse children. In most cases, she says, the abusers were abused children. "Often we learn how to be good parents by remembering

Many children deal with their pain alone rather than tell anyone about the abuses they suffer.

how our parents treated us," she says. "Unfortunately, the reverse is true, too."[19]

A twenty-one-year-old mother of two agrees. As a little girl, she was the target of name-calling and other abuse by her father. She says that she hated it. She vowed she would never do that to her own children when she grew up. But now, she admits, she has to stop herself from saying mean things when her children misbehave.

"I called my daughter a name a few weeks ago, and she looked so shocked," she says. "I was shocked, too. It just came out of my mouth. It was a name my father used to call me! Without thinking, I just said it. I guess you never forget your childhood."[20]

Chapter Four

Fighting Against Abuse

Child abuse is complicated. Fighting child abuse is not an easy task. For one thing, the victims are often too young to speak up. Even older children often keep abuse in their families a secret. But many people are working to end child abuse. And while they are working toward the same goal, they work on many different parts of the problem.

Identifying Abuse

The most important first step is to stop abuse that is happening now. Identifying abused children has always been difficult. Physically abused children have burns, broken bones, or bruises. However, children can receive these injuries in accidents, too. How do doctors know if injuries are from abuse or accidents?

Over the past twenty years, doctors have learned a great deal about abuse. "We know a thousand times more than we did twenty years ago," says one doctor, "and ten times more than we did ten years ago."[21] They have found that certain kinds of injuries are much more likely to be caused by abuse

A victim of abuse, who was set on fire when he was a child, shares his story on a television talk show.

than by an accident. A doctor who sees such injuries knows that it is likely that the child is abused.

Doctors are suspicious when a child's medical chart shows a history of bruises—especially on areas other than arms and legs. Burns, too, are worrisome. Emergency room workers know they must listen carefully when a parent explains how the burns occurred. They need to look carefully at the child, to see if the injuries match the story.

One babysitter's story did not match a child's burns. The woman said that the little girl burned herself by accidentally turning on the hot water in the bathtub. But the doctors saw that the baby's red, burned skin came up to an even ring around her stomach. That showed she had been dipped—and held down—in the steaming water.

Looking for Shaken Babies

One cause of serious injuries is known as **shaken baby syndrome**. One mother brought her baby to

A wall of hands was raised in 2002 to remember children who have died of abuse in Massachusetts.

the emergency room. She said that the baby fell out of his crib. The doctor noted that the baby seemed half-awake and was having difficulty breathing. Alarmed, the doctor checked for bleeding inside the baby's eye, in a part called the **retina**.

Seeing that there was bleeding, the doctor knew right away that the mother was not telling the truth. The little boy had not fallen from his crib. He had most likely been shaken very hard—perhaps because he had been crying. The shaking had injured the baby's brain and caused his retinas to bleed.

Shaking a baby is very, very dangerous. One doctor says that the thought of it is frightening. "For me, shaken baby syndrome is the worst thing," she says, "because in a matter of moments, a healthy baby is dead or severely disabled for life."[22]

What Then?

But what happens when it is clear that a child has been abused? A teacher, daycare worker, or doctor who suspects abuse will call the police or a family services worker. They determine how serious the problem is. In cases of extreme abuse, where the child's life is in danger, the abuser is arrested.

One woman says that her boyfriend was arrested and put in jail. "Terry hit my daughter over and over with a belt," she says. "I wasn't home, I didn't know about it. But at school the girl's teacher noticed right away. That teacher called the police. And they took him to jail. I won't have any more to do with him."[23]

Another mother's children were taken from her by family services. "The lady from family services took my kids to a shelter," she says. "That was the third time I got arrested for selling [crack]. It was hard on me, hard on the girls, too. At the time I was really mad. I thought, how can they just come and get my kids? But I look back, and I know I'd do the same thing if I was family service. How could they leave those little kids with me, when I was a strung-out **junkie?**"[24]

A member of the Children's Trust Fund of Alabama gathers pinwheels as part of a campaign to promote child abuse awareness.

The goal is not to punish the parents or frighten the child. It is to keep the child away until the counselors can learn what is happening in the family. Sometimes a parent is abusing drugs or alcohol and needs help. Or a parent is under a great deal of stress. The family services workers may decide that the child is not safe in the home. They might move the child to an emergency shelter, or a **foster home**, until the problem is solved.

President Bill Clinton signs the Child Abuse Protection and Enforcement Act in 2000.

Preventing Abuse

Many programs help parents who are abusers. Counselors teach mothers and fathers to discipline without hitting or yelling. They explain how abuse affects children. They sometimes do role-playing games. The counselor pretends to be the parent, and the parent pretends to be the child. The parents realize what it feels like to be threatened and called names. One father said that the class changed him.

"I've learned so much," says Ray, a formerly abusive father. "I know I'm a better dad than I ever was. I feel ashamed when I think of all the shouting and name-calling I did, and the slapping. My kids are young. I'm hoping they forget how I used to be. I'm never being that way again."[25]

Another help in preventing abuse is the **crisis nursery**. It is a twenty-four-hour center where stressed-out parents can drop off their children *before* the parents lose their tempers. One mother had a bad headache and her children were being noisy. She asked them to be quiet, but they did not listen. She knew that she was close to hitting them. Instead, she drove them to the nursery, where they were looked after until she felt better. Many communities around the country have opened crisis nurseries, with good results.

Many Ways to Solve a Problem

Child abuse is a dangerous problem. But it is important to know that many people are working to

Children who grow up in concerned, loving families are more likely to grow into healthy adults.

solve the problem. Some are finding better ways to identify abused children. Some are working to repair the damage abuse does. Some people are working with abusers, getting them to change their behavior.

All of these people are working on different parts of the problem. But they all believe the same thing: No child deserves to be hurt or neglected.

Notes

Chapter One: A National Disgrace

1. Interview with the author, January 1990, Minneapolis, Minnesota.
2. Carol Ott, telephone interview, August 1996.
3. Mary, interview with the author, April 1997, Maple Grove, Minnesota.
4. Tony, interview with the author, October 1997, Minneapolis, Minnesota.
5. Ott interview.

Chapter Two: Why Do They Do It?

6. Interview with the author, August 1996, Minneapolis, Minnesota.
7. Lisa, interview with the author, April 1997, Richfield, Minnesota.
8. Interview with the author, April 1997, St. Paul, Minnesota.
9. Trina, interview with the author, August 1995, Minneapolis, Minnesota.
10. Jane Kreuger, telephone interview, July 1989.
11. Dorie, interview with the author, February 1997, Inver Grove Heights, Minnesota.

Chapter Three: "You Never Forget"

12. Quoted in Bob Greene, "What Happened to Joseph," *Life*, March 1, 2000, p. 37.
13. Kadee, interview with the author, May 1996, Minneapolis, Minnesota.
14. Jerry, interview with the author, September 1997, Plymouth, Minnesota.

15. Allie, interview with the author, January 1999, Minneapolis, Minnesota.
16. Jenny, interview with the author, January 1997, St. Paul, Minnesota.
17. Interview with the author, January 1996, Minneapolis, Minnesota.
18. Telephone interview with the author, January 2002.
19. Kreuger interview.
20. Interview with the author, June 1997, Minneapolis, Minnesota.

Chapter Four: Fighting Against Abuse
21. Quoted in Arthur Allen, "She Catches Child Abusers," *Redbook*, March 1999, p. 118.
22. Quoted in Allen, "She Catches Child Abusers," p. 118.
23. Interview with the author, March 1997, Robbinsdale, Minnesota.
24. Interview with the author, September 1996, Minneapolis, Minnesota.
25. Ray, interview with the author, January 2001, Minneapolis, Minnesota.

Glossary

child abuse: Hurting a child in any way that will cause injury.

crack: A form of the drug cocaine, which is very addictive.

crisis nursery: A twenty-four-hour, drop-in child center for parents who might abuse their children.

foster home: A temporary home for children whose own homes are unsafe.

junkie: A slang term for a drug addict.

neglect: A form of abuse in which a child is ignored and not cared for.

retina: A part of the inner eye that is often injured when a baby is shaken.

shaken baby syndrome: A life-threatening type of abuse that causes brain injuries.

therapist: A person who works with people who need to change their behavior. Therapists can help both abusers and the victims of abuse.

For Further Exploration

Books

Deborah Anderson, *Michael's Story: Emotional Abuse and Working with a Counselor.* Minneapolis: Dillon Press, 1986. Short, very readable account of a boy who was emotionally abused, and his work with a counselor trying to help him.

Carolyn Coman, *What Jamie Saw.* Arden, NC: Front Street, 1995. Story about a nine-year-old victim of abuse, and the way he is dealing with his fears.

Susan Mufson, *Straight Talk About Child Abuse.* New York: Facts On File, 1991. Suitable for advanced readers, with good examples of types of abuse.

Websites

Child Abuse Prevention Network (www.child-abuse.com). An organization providing support and educational materials for all people who are working either to prevent child abuse or to treat the victims of child abuse.

Childhelp USA (www.childhelpusa.org). An organization that focuses efforts and resources on the treatment and prevention of child abuse.

Index

abusers
  background of,
    30–32
  described, 13
alcohol abuse, 9
Allie, 26–28
anger, 11, 13–14

beatings, 9, 14
bruises
  from kicking, 24
  from slapping, 5
  from whipping, 14, 23,
    26
burns, 16, 34–35

cases reported, 6, 12
causes, 11, 13–14
cost, 9
counselors
  abusers and, 31–32
  prevention and, 39
  at shelters, 10–11
crack addiction, 16–18, 37
crisis nurseries, 39

deaths, 6
definition, 6

doctors, 33–36
Dorie, 20–22
drug addiction, 16–18,
  37

effects
  emotional, 10–11,
    28–30, 32
  physical, 5, 14, 16, 23,
    24, 26, 33–36

fear, 25–26
foster homes, 26, 38

homeless teenagers, 28

identification, 33–36

Jan, 4–6
Jenny, 28

kicking, 23–24

Lee, 8–9
Lisa, 14

Mark, 4–5

Mary, 8–9

name-calling, 32
neglect, 16–18, 20–22, 26

physical abuse
  beating, 9, 14
  burning, 16, 34–35
  identification of, 33–36
  kicking, 23–24
  pinching, 9
  slapping, 4–5
  whipping, 23, 26
pinching, 9
prevention, 39

Ray, 39

runaways, 28

self-esteem, 30
shaken baby syndrome, 35–36
shelters, 9–10, 26, 37, 38
slapping, 4–5

Ted, 6–8
teenagers
  homeless, 28
  mothers, 18, 20–22
Terry, 36–37
therapists, 10–11
threats, 26
Tony, 9–10
trust, 29–30

whippings, 23, 26

Picture Credits

About the Author

Gail B. Stewart has written over ninety books for young people, including a series for Lucent Books called The Other America. She has written many books on historical topics such as World War I and the Warsaw ghetto.

Stewart received her undergraduate degree from Gustavus Adolphus College in St. Peter, Minnesota. She did her graduate work in English, linguistics, and curriculum study at the College of St. Thomas and the University of Minnesota. She taught English and reading for more than ten years. Stewart and her husband live in Minneapolis with their three sons.